CW00820533

For Isabella & Sophie

xxx

Stuart the Wrestling Seal

Written by Janek Puzon

Illustrated by Christina Collins

Stuart the seal was a regular pup,
He had a dream for when he grew up.
While his friends wanted to be singers,
astronauts and vets,
Stuart had the strangest vocation yet.

"I'm going to be a wrestler, just you wait and see,"
Vowed Stuart quietly to himself with glee.
He doodled and drew himself in wrestler's clothes,
with a big blue cape and a mask on his nose.
But all his friends laughed and said with a sneer,
"A wrestler? A wrestler? What a silly idea!"

**"Hear us all, hear us all, hear us all sing,
For how can a seal be a wrestling king?!"**

"I'll show them" said Stuart as he ran
home from school,
"I'll show them that wrestling is both
fun and cool."

**"They will all, they will all, they will all sing,
that Stuart the seal is a wrestling king!"**

Stuart thought for a moment on the
outfit he could wear,
But his cupboards were empty and his
wardrobe was bare.
So he tried his parent's room for
things he could find,
"I can borrow mum and dad's things,
I'm sure they won't mind."

Stuart found a blue coat he could use as his cape,
And over his shoulders did his mum's blue coat drape.
He found a pair of his dad's socks even though they were smelly,
"This will do as a mask, I'll look good on the telly."

Stuart then put on his mum's glittery, feather boa,
"My mum will love this, I can't wait to show her."
And then quite suddenly, Stuart's parents returned home,
"They'll love this outfit when they see me perform."

"Ta da!" said Stuart, "look at my wrestling clothes!"
As he spun around and perfomed a confident pose.
"I'm going to be a wrestler and this is my costume,"
Said Stuart as he strutted up and down the living room.

His parents then paused and looked at each other,
Before laughing uproariously, both father and mother.
A wrestler?" shrieked his dad and with nothing to lose,
Declared, "You can barely tie the laces of your own shoes!"
His mother then added, "You should be outside flying kites,
Not grappling with others, whilst wearing my tights!"

**"Hear us both, hear us both, hear us both sing,
For how can a seal be a wrestling king?!"**

Stuart was devastated and he ran far away,
"People can hurt with the things that they say.
I don't want a job farming or writing cheques,
I want to perform slams and perfect my suplex!
I can show everyone the skills that I'll accrue,
I can trash talk the bad guys and show what I can do.

They will all, they will all, they will all sing,
That Stuart the seal is a wrestling king!"

Stuart was upset and went into the woods,
Which was at the other side of the neighbourhood.
He wanted some time away on his own,
"After this, I'll go back," he said with a moan.

After some time, Stuart decided to go back;
He didn't want to become someone else's snack.
He went down a left and then up a right,
He had to hurry up while the sky was still light.

"This bridge isn't familiar,
It's not one I have crossed."
It was here that Stuart knew he
was completely lost.
Stuart cried out for help,
hoping somebody heard,
There was nobody nearby, not
even a bird.

And then came a rustle from the nearest bush,
Over the area descended a hush.
"Who is there?" requested a shadowy figure,
Stuart showed no fear and approached it with vigour.
"I am Stuart the seal, a wrestling god!"
He confidently said, with the cape on his bod .
And with his eyes peering through his dad's smelly old sock,
Stuart said, "I can put you in the figure four leg-lock!"

"Wooah there kid," said the mysterious shape,
As he eyeballed the seal in the big, blue cape.
"I am Bruno the bear and I pose no threat,
I reckon you're lost, on that I can bet."

"Although I am big and although I am bad,
You are safe from harm, I guarantee that young lad.
And from your trash talk, I would like to state,
That you must be a wrestler, am I right, mate?"

Stuart was relieved and also taken aback,
That the figure in front wouldn't give him a whack.

Didn't he say he thought Stuart was a wrestler too?
A compliment! That surely deserves a **Woooo!**

Stuart asked, "How do you know
what a wrestler sounds like?"
Bruno replied, "Because you'd sound
dynamite with a mic!
I was a wrestler back in the day,
I know a wrestler when I see one,
I'd say."

Stuart was speechless, he knew this
was his chance.
He uttered the next words, even
though in a trance;
"Would you train me to wrestle and
become the best?
I think I have what it takes to pass
the test!"

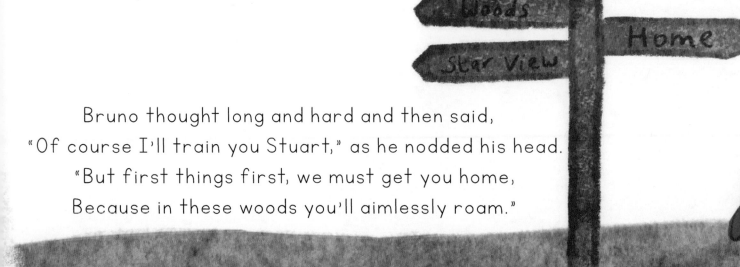

Bruno thought long and hard and then said,
"Of course I'll train you Stuart," as he nodded his head.
"But first things first, we must get you home,
Because in these woods you'll aimlessly roam."

"Come back tomorrow, straight after school,
And I'll teach you to wrestle and then you will rule."
Bruno helped Stuart find the right track,
And before you knew it, Stuart was back.

His parents asked him where he had been,
And Stuart told them about what he had seen.
"We're sorry we laughed Stuart, you know we love you,
We're just not sure wrestling is the thing to do."
"This is my dream Mum and Dad, Bruno can help,
I will drop kick and make my opponents yelp!"
His parents decided to then make a deal,
That Bruno could give wrestling lessons to the daft, young seal.

Stuart was excited and as he went to bed,
A chant reverberated over and over in his head.

**"They will all, they will all, they will all sing,
That Stuart the seal is a wrestling king!"**

Stuart got straight into the groove,
And thought about what would be his signature move.
He said his goodbyes to both mum and dad,
The thought of wrestling lessons made him wonderfully glad.

The school day went past in a bit of a blur,
Stuart thought of Bruno and chest chops to his fur.
Once the school bell sounded, Stuart was off like a shot,
To learn about wrestling and make the crowd say

'What?!'

Once there, Bruno put Stuart through his paces,
With his wrestling trunks on and his big boots with laces.
"Come on Stuart, that headlock's too weak,
You'd struggle against the likes of
The Big Camel Sheikh!"

Over the next few weeks
Stuart learned more and more;
He paced matches better,
sweating from every pore.

He even learned how to
wax Bruno's car,
Though he suspected
that a joke that had
gone too far.

His friendship with Bruno continued to bloom,
He learned of Bruno's rivalvry with Dave 'Meerkat' Doom.
"Dave was nasty and a big bad bully,
He picked on The Frogmeister and Steve 'Squirrel-Man' Sully."

"The last I heard he was doing time inside,
For stealing some money, or at least he had tried.
He was the only wrestler I did not defeat;
I'd have loved the crowd to have greeted him with 'Delete!'"

As the weeks went on, Stuart continued to believe,
That his wrestling goals were something to achieve.

**"They will all, they will all, they will all sing,
That Stuart the seal is a wrestling king!"**

Then during one lesson,
Bruno presented a gift,
And this sure gave Stuart a big confidence lift.
"This is the wrestling outfit in which I'd appear,
In this I spilled blood, sweat and tears."

"This is yours now, to your success it is vital,
I hope it helps you win the World Wildlife Title!"
Stuart was shocked as he received the suprise,
It brought goosebumps to his skin and tears to his eyes.

"Oh thank you, oh thank you, oh thank you!" he said,
As he admired the yellow boots and tights that were red.
"You've earned it Stuart, through all your hard work,
Carry on with your efforts, those that you mustn't shirk."

Stuart ran home, as proud as can be,
"Wait til mum and dad get a good look at me!"
He burst through the door to let them both look,
At the clothing from Bruno he excitedly took.
"Here I am, Stuart the wrestling seal!" he said,
"I'll deliver clotheslines and put a lock on your head!"
Stuart waited for a reply off them both,
Yet the response he received was something he'd loathe.

"Not again with all these wrestling wishes,
It's your time to wash and then dry the dishes!"
Stuart was upset and he ran to his bed,
"I just want the chance to prove them wrong," he said.
Stuart knew with his newfound talent,
He'd prove he was worthy and extremely gallant.

**"They will all, they will all, they will all sing,
That Stuart the seal is a wrestling king!"**

Stuart fell asleep in his wrestling gear,
Dreaming of slams and performing a spear.
When from downstairs came an awful din,
That made Stuart jump right out of his wrestler's skin!

The noise was so loud, there was somebody there,
That made the hairs stand up on Stuart's silvery fur.
Instead of being frightened, Stuart thought it best,
To investigate who had interrupted his rest.

Stuart heard the noise coming straight from
the kitchen;
To get his hands on the foe, Stuart was itchin'.
He quietly made his way to the noise,
With his wrestling lock up ready,
Stuart was poised.

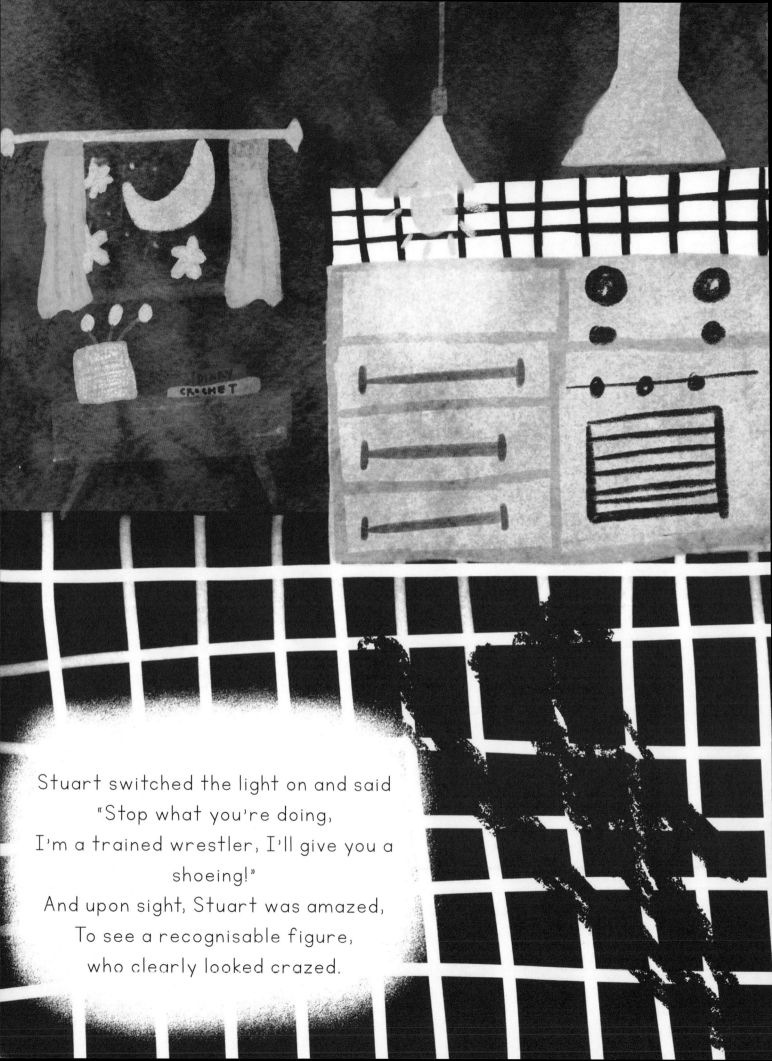

Stuart switched the light on and said
"Stop what you're doing,
I'm a trained wrestler, I'll give you a
shoeing!"
And upon sight, Stuart was amazed,
To see a recognisable figure,
who clearly looked crazed.

"You're no wrestler, compared to me,
I'll leave this house a big pile of debris.
I have beaten the best and now I'll beat you!"
Shrieked the figure before Stuart, ready to lock up he was too.

It was the meerkat that Bruno had told him about,
And before you knew it, Stuart gave him a clout.
"Take that, Dave 'Meerkat' Doom,
As that is who you are, I assume?"

Dave dropped to the floor like a
bag of cement,
This was the moment for which
Stuart was meant.

"I am Stuart the wrestling seal,"
he announced,

And straight after that, it was
Stuart who pounced.

"This is my signature move you scrubber!
I call it the 'Seal Hold of Blubber!' "
Stuart then grabbed Dave's legs in a hold,
And bent them to places they should just not fold.
"Arrggghhh!" screamed Dave as loud as he could,
"Get off me, get off me, if you kindly would?"
But Stuart did not let go of big Dave's legs,
Ignoring the sounds of his high-pitched begs.

Then in burst Stuart's parents to see what was occurring,
To see what incident caused them to be stirring.
The sight of Stuart making a meerkat cry,
Was the craziest thing they'd seen, they couldn't deny.

"Call the police Dad, this meerkat's had enough displeasure,
Unless he wants an elbow drop for good measure?"
"No get off me please, I give up!"
Wept Dave as he submitted to the brave, young pup.

The police arrived and
took Dave Doom away,
For a long time in prison,
the meerkat would stay.

"Well done young fella,"
the policeman said,
"He'll spend a good few nights
in a hospital bed!"

Stuart's parents were proud of what their son had done,
It was his first and only bout he had won.
"Wrestling is what you were born to do,"
Said his mum and dad and they knew this to be true.

They hugged him and wiped their tears away,
Their love for him stronger than Dave's legs that gave way.
"I told you that wrestling was something I could do!"
"You did son and we should have listened to you."

The next day, word had gotten around school,
About how Stuart made Dave Doom look a fool.
All the pupils, even the teachers there,
Wanted Stuart's story, who, what and where?!

But best of all was yet to come,
After school, Stuart caught sight of his
dad and his mum.
And not only that, Bruno was there too,
"Well done Stuart, we're so proud of you!"
All pupils, parents and Bruno were there,
To raise Stuart up, high into the air.

"Hear us all, hear us all, hear us all sing,
For Stuart the seal is a wrestling king!"

About the Author

Janek Puzon is a husband and father of two young girls whose passion for writing was rekindled during his return to education when completing a Community Coaching and Sports Development degree as well as a PostGraduate Certificate in Education qualification.

Janek, however, has never been a wrestler.

Printed in Great Britain
by Amazon

83977472R00033